RUPERT
AND THE SECRET BOAT

Written by
MIKE TRUMBLE

Based on a story by Alfred Bestall MBE

GUILD PUBLISHING   LONDON

This edition published 1989
by Guild Publishing
by arrangement with BBC Books

First published 1989

CN 4302

Rupert Bear and Characters
© Express Newspapers Plc 1989

Text © Michael Trumble and
Express Newspapers Plc 1989

Typeset in Plantin 12/14 pt.
by Keyspools Ltd, Warrington

Colour separations by Dot Gradations Ltd, Chelmsford
Printed in Great Britain by Cambus Litho, East Kilbride
Cover printed by Fletchers of Norwich

Rupert's gone to the seaside with Gregory,
His little guineapig chum.
"How sunny it is," says Rupert happily,
"We've chosen the right day to come."

And as they both explore the sandy beach,
They see their friend the Professor,
"I'm about to try my secret boat," he says,
"It has an electric motor.

I've asked my assistant to take the boat
To those rocks, just over there,"
The kind old Professor carefully explains
To Gregory and Rupert Bear.

"And it's from up here that I'll control it
With this transmitter radio."
Just then the Professor's assistant returns
And says the boat's all set to go.

"May we ride in your boat," asks Gregory,
"On its first journey on the sea?"
The Professor says that of course they can,
Which fills them both with glee.

So they follow the Professor's assistant
Down a path to the secret boat;
With care they climb into the little craft
And smoothly out to sea they float.

"The Professor's clever to build this boat
And control it with a radio,"
Says the little bear as further out to sea
The two very happy chums go.

It's a marvellous trip for both of them
And they're having lots of fun
As the gentle waves rock them off to sleep
Beneath the very warm sun.

But a voice calling, "Hello sleepyheads,
  You must wake up! Ahoy there!"
Gives Rupert and Gregory quite a start
  And awakens the dozing pair.

"Merboy, why are you here at the seaside?"
  Asks Rupert, and the Merboy smiles,
"Little bear, this is where I live," he says,
  "Your boat's drifted many miles."

"My goodness, Merboy's right," gasps Rupert,
"Those are tropical islands, Gregory!"
"Well I hope there's food there," says Gregory,
"I'm feeling rather hungry."

The Professor has lost control of the boat,
Now it's drifted out of reach.
So the Merboy helps by pushing the craft
To the nearest island's beach.

On the small island the chums eat fresh fruit
Until they can eat no more,
And as the little guineapig sleeps again,
Rupert sets off to explore.

He hasn't gone far when he sees a big cave
At the end of a narrow track.
The brave little bear enters, trips over
And slides down a slope on his back.

As he's about to plunge into deep water
He feels something grab him,
"Phew, saved!" sighs the little bear with relief,
"That could have been very grim."

Gently, Rupert's lifted up high,
Then set down upon a damp rock,
But when Rupert sees what has just saved him,
He feels quite ill with shock.

In front of him stands a giant sea serpent
With a very frightening frown,
"Thankyou for s-s-saving m-m-me," he says,
"I didn't want to d-d-drown."

"What are you doing on my island, little bear?"
The great beast roars angrily,
"Our b-b-boat d-d-drifted h-h-here,"
Rupert replies nervously.

And, as he thinks he's about to end up
As the sea serpent's supper,
Up from the bottom of the dark deep water
Pops the great monster's youngster.

"My, what a small bear," cries the baby serpent,
"I've never seen such a small one!
Oh please will you let me keep him, Mother,
I'm sure he'll be great fun."

"I'm s-s-sorry," says Rupert bravely,
"But I really can't s-s-stay,
You see I'm only here at the seaside,
With my chum, for just one day."

"You're a brave little bear," says the serpent,
"I didn't mean to cause alarm.
My son will show you the way out of our cave,
And he'll keep you safe from harm."

"I can help you find your boat, little bear,
You could be searching all night."
Says the young sea serpent as he leads Rupert
Out of the cave into warm sunlight.

"Now I wonder where on earth Gregory can be?"
Says the concerned little bear.
"Let me ride on your shoulder," squawks a parrot,
"I know and I'll show you where."

And, sure enough, it leads the way to Gregory
Who's picking fruit from the trees.
"Rupert," he cries as he spies the sea serpent,
"Don't come any closer please!"

"Don't be so frightened, Gregory," calls Rupert,
"This young sea serpent's a chum,
And he's going to help us to find our boat,
That's the only reason he's come.

He really won't harm you," says the little bear,
"All he wants to do is play.
Come on, we must hurry and find the boat
Which I think is over that way."

They go the way he points, and find the boat
Bobbing on the incoming tide,
"I've never been in a boat," says the serpent,
"Please may I come for the ride?"

So along with the sea serpent and parrot too,
They return to the seaside bay;
When the Professor's assistant sees the serpent
He cries, "Oh no!" and runs away.

He comes back with the Professor, who's pleased
To see that both the chums are there.
"Where on earth did you get to?" he asks them,
"We've been looking for you everywhere."

So Rupert tells him all about the island
To which the two of them have been,
How they met the young sea serpent and parrot,
And about the fruit trees they've seen.

And as Rupert's two new friends return home
To the island across the sea,
The little bear cries, "See you soon, I hope!"
As he waves goodbye happily.